FIRST STEPS IN SCIENCE

WHAT IS MOTION?
A CYCLING ADVENTURE

BY KAY BARNHAM AND MARCELO BADARI

WAYLAND

First published in Great Britain in 2023
by Wayland
Copyright © Hodder and Stoughton, 2023

All rights reserved

Editor: Grace Glendinning
Cover design concept: Peter Scoulding
Cover and inside design: Emma DeBanks

HB ISBN: 978 1 5263 2018 6
PB ISBN: 978 1 5263 2019 3

Printed and bound in China

Wayland, an imprint of
Hachette Children's Group
Part of Hodder and Stoughton
Carmelite House
50 Victoria Embankment
London EC4Y 0DZ

An Hachette UK Company
www.hachette.co.uk
www.hachettechildrens.co.uk

OXFORDSHIRE COUNTY COUNCIL	
3303774129	
Askews & Holts	13-Feb-2023
P531.11 JUNIOR NON-F	

FSC® C104740
MIX Paper from responsible sources

The website addresses (URLs) included in this book were valid at the time of going to press. However, it is possible that contents or addresses may have changed since the publication of this book. No responsibility for any such changes can be accepted by either the author or the Publisher.

WHAT IS MOTION?

Let's find out! Join super-sporty robots Flex and Flash on a cycling adventure that's sure to be filled with ups and downs. We'll learn some fabulous facts about **motion** on the way. Let's go, super-scientists!

Flex and Flash can run so fast that the world becomes a blur.

Flex

Flash

They can use a l-o-o-o-o-o-o-n-g bendy pole to vault high into the air.

And when the weather is freezing cold, they s-l-i-i-i-i-i-i-i-i-i-i-i-i-d-e on ice skates.

s-l-i-i-i-i-i-i-i-i-i-i-i-i-i-i-i-i-i-i-d-e

s-l-i-i-i-i-i-i-i-i-i-i-i-i-i-i-i-i-i-i-i-i-i-i-d-e

But what Flex and Flash like to do most of all is whizz along on their super-cycles!

whizzzzzz

whizzzzzz

The robots have pumped up their tyres and checked their brakes. They're ready for a great cycling adventure.

Wait for me!

Flex and Flash push their pedals round to make their bicycles move forwards. The super-robots are in motion!

Let's go!

Motion is what happens when anything moves.

The cycle path is wide and flat. It's the perfect place for the robots to have a race!

Ready... Steady... GO!

BEEP-DEE-BOOP

Flash sets off slowly. He whistles a tune as he cycles.

But Flex pedals hard. His super-robot feet turn the pedals round and round and round. He's going faster than Flash.

Speed tells us how quickly – or how slowly – something is going.

The two robots are travelling at very different speeds!

peeeeo

Flex is still in the lead!

But what's this? Flash is pedalling much harder now. He's speeding up. When he cycles downhill, he goes faster still!

If something starts to go faster, its speed **increases**. This is called **acceleration**.

Ooowwww!

Oh no! Flex's battery is getting low. He's going slower and s-l-o-w-e-r.

Deceleration is another way of saying that speed is **decreasing** (going more slowly). It's the **opposite** of acceleration.

Flash whizzes past. Now *he's* in the lead!
Hooray! Flash is the winner!

Well done, Flash!

After a quick recharge, Flex has a full battery and is ready to roll again!

Flex and Flash have reached the off-road cycle track. Now they can try all different types of motion!

The super-robots ride over the ENORMOUS bumps.

UP

DOWN

Motion isn't always in a straight line. It can go in many **directions**, such as up and down.

UP

DOWN

They go UP and DOWN and UP and DOWN so many times that they feel as if they are on springs!

15

When Flex and Flash rattle over the rough and rocky ground, they are still going up and down, but the up-and-down movements are VERY SMALL.

All of the super-robots' nuts and bolts jangle and shake. Their heads wobble side to side, back and forth, over and over and over! That's a lot of motion!

Squawk Squawk

What other up-and-down and side-to-side motions do you see around you each day?

The curved banks on the trail are super-awesome. It's like riding inside a bowl! As the super-robots whizz round, their bikes begin to tip over ... but they don't fall!

I can see the park!

It's a non-stop adventure!

Forces keep the super-cyclists glued to their bikes – and their bikes glued to the path – when they ride fast in a circular motion.

I wonder if we'll find any new types of motion at the park?

There's only one way to find out!

FORWARDS

UP   UP

The super-robots SLIDE FORWARDS along the zip wire.

They clamber UP the climbing frame.

UP

DOWN

They go UP and DOWN and UP and DOWN and UP and DOWN on the seesaw.

ROUND

ROUND

They whirl ROUND and ROUND and ROUND on the spinner. Hold tight, robots!

Flex and Flash save the best for last.
They LOVE the swings! The super-robots
will take turns pushing each other.
Flash pushes first.

wheeeeeeee!

Flex flies forwards through the air ...
and then backwards again. Wheeeeeee!

It's hard work. Flash soon needs a break and he stops pushing. But Flex is still swinging!

WHY?

If an object is moving, then it has **momentum**. It will carry on moving until a force – like **gravity** or a strong robot friend – makes it stop.

Flex and Flash have so much fun that the afternoon speeds past. Suddenly, they notice that the Sun is setting. Oh dear.

They're going to be late!

whhhoosh!

But the super-robots have a brilliant idea. Instead of cycling back, they switch on their ROCKET POWER.

Cars, trains, boats, aeroplanes, rockets and sometimes robot feet have **engines** inside them. This means they can move quickly. The more powerful the engine, the faster the vehicle can go.

Flex and Flash fly so fast that the journey home takes no time at all.

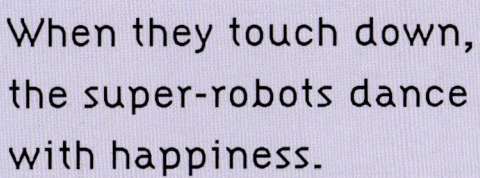

When they touch down, the super-robots dance with happiness.

Dancing is a type of motion too! It puts together lots of different motions in one.

It's the perfect way to end a motion-packed day.

It's time to dance! Can YOU create a dance routine that uses all of these different types of motion?

Jumping

Running around in circles

Spinning

Swinging your arms

Running forwards

Sliding

Kicking

Twisting

Stepping forwards

GLOSSARY

Acceleration: when something goes faster

Deceleration: when something goes slower

Decreasing: getting smaller and smaller or less and less

Direction: the way something goes

Engine: a machine that makes things move

Force: a push or a pull

Gravity: the force that pulls things towards Earth

Increases: grows or gets bigger

Momentum: a measurement of a moving object's strength; heavier objects have more momentum

Motion: the amount of movement that something has

Opposite: when one thing is as different as it can be from another, for example: fast and slow are opposite to each other

Speed: how quickly or slowly something moves

GUIDE FOR TEACHERS, PARENTS AND CARERS

This book can help young children to learn about motion – one of the concepts that form the foundation of physics. They may then begin to understand how the world and everything in it works.

Motion is what happens when something moves. Forces can make objects move, speed up, slow down and change direction.

In this book, readers find out how motion works in real-life contexts, through the eyes of two awesome cycling robots! Readers may then go on to discover new examples for themselves in their own lives.

FURTHER INFORMATION

To find out more about motion, why not visit one of these terrific museums?

The Science Museum, London
www.sciencemuseum.org.uk

The National Railway Museum, York
www.railwaymuseum.org.uk

Royal Air Force Museum, Cosford
www.rafmuseum.org.uk

INDEX

A
acceleration 11–12

D
dancing 27–29
deceleration 12

E
engines 25

F
forces 19, 23

G
gravity 23

M
momentum 23
motion 3, 6–7, 14–17, 19–29

S
speed 9–12, 25